D0730769

...er
...e

...each Penguin Young Readers book is assigned a traditional easy-to-read level (1–4) as well as a Guided Reading Level (A–P). Both of these systems will help you choose the right book for your child. Please refer to the back of each book for specific leveling information. Penguin Young Readers features esteemed authors and illustrators, stories about favorite characters, fascinating nonfiction, and more!

Cork and Fuzz: Finders Keepers

LEVEL **3**

GUIDED READING LEVEL **J**

This book is perfect for a **Transitional Reader** who:
• can read multisyllable and compound words;
• can read words with prefixes and suffixes;
• is able to identify story elements (beginning, middle, end, plot, setting, characters, problem, solution); and
• can understand different points of view.

DISCARDS

Here are some **activities** you can do during and after reading this book:
• Character Traits: Cork and Fuzz are best friends, but they are very different. On a separate piece of paper, write a list of words that describe Cork. Then write a list of words that describe Fuzz.
• Story Map: A story map is a visual organizer that helps you understand what happens in a story. On a separate piece of paper, create a story map for *Finders Keepers*. The map should include: Setting (where and when each story takes place), Characters (who is in the story), Problem (the difficulty or problem in this story), Goal (what the characters want to happen), Events (list three things that happened in the story that helped the characters reach their goal), and Ending (the solution—how the characters solved the problem and achieved their goal).

Remember, sharing the love of reading with a child is the best gift you can give!

—Bonnie Bader, EdM
  Penguin Young Readers program

*Penguin Young Readers are leveled by independent reviewers applying the standards developed by Irene Fountas and Gay Su Pinnell in *Matching Books to Readers: Using Leveled Books in Guided Reading*, Heinemann, 1999.

For Nicki,
finder and keeper of small things—DC

To my husband, Ken,
I found you, and you're a keeper!—LM

PENGUIN YOUNG READERS
Published by the Penguin Group
Penguin Group (USA) Inc., 375 Hudson Street, New York, New York 10014, USA

USA | Canada | UK | Ireland | Australia | New Zealand | India | South Africa | China
Penguin Books Ltd, Registered Offices: 80 Strand, London WC2R 0RL, England

For more information about the Penguin Group visit penguin.com

Text copyright © 2009 by Dori Chaconas. Illustrations copyright © 2009 by Lisa McCue. All rights reserved. First published in 2009 by Viking, an imprint of Penguin Group (USA) Inc. Published in 2013 by Penguin Young Readers, an imprint of Penguin Group (USA) Inc., 345 Hudson Street, New York, New York 10014. Manufactured in China.

The Library of Congress has cataloged the Viking edition under the following Control Number:
2008021551

ISBN 978-0-14-241869-7   10 9 8 7 6 5 4 3

ALWAYS LEARNING   PEARSON

CORK & FUZZ

Finders Keepers

by Dori Chaconas
illustrated by Lisa McCue

Penguin Young Readers
An Imprint of Penguin Group (USA) Inc.

Chapter 1

Cork was a short muskrat.

He liked to find things.

He liked to find soft feathers,

smooth sticks, and shiny stones.

Fuzz was a tall possum.

He liked to keep things.

He liked to keep food in his mouth,

jokes in his head,

and sometimes someone else's things.

Two best friends.

Kind of the same, but different.

One day Cork found

a shiny green stone.

It was the best stone!

He threw it up in the air.

He caught it.

He threw it in the air again.

And then he lost it.

"Oh no!" he said.

He looked in the grass.

He looked in the ferns.

He looked in the bushes.

But he could not find

his new green stone.

Fuzz came running.

"Cork! Cork!" Fuzz called.

"Hurry! Come to my yard!

I have found something!"

"I have lost something!" Cork said.

"I have lost my best green stone."

"How did you lose it?" Fuzz asked.

"I was throwing it up in the air,"
Cork said.

"I was catching it.

I missed!

Now I cannot find it."

Fuzz looked down at his feet.

He bent over.

He picked up a shiny green stone.

"Look what I found!" Fuzz said.

"I found a green stone."

"That is the stone I lost!" Cork said.

"Finders keepers," Fuzz said.

"But that is my best stone!"
Cork said.

"Will you give it back to me?"

"I will think about it," Fuzz said.

"But first come to my yard.
Come and see what I have found!"

Chapter 2

"What did you find?" Cork asked.

"I found a lump in my yard!"
Fuzz said.

"There are a lot of lumps in your
yard," Cork said.

"Can I have my stone back?"
Fuzz held the stone tighter.

"I did not find an old lump," Fuzz said.

"I found a new lump!"

"What does it look like?" Cork asked.

"And can I have my stone back, *please*?"

"It is a hidden lump," Fuzz said.

"It is hidden under a pile of leaves."

"Maybe it is only a lump of leaves,"
Cork said.

"And *please*, *please*, *PLEASE* can I have
my stone?"

Fuzz held the stone behind his back.

"It is not only a lump of leaves!" Fuzz
said.

"There is something under the
leaves.

It makes a strange noise."

"Do you think you have found
something dangerous?" Cork asked.

Fuzz's eyes opened wide.

"We will take a big, long stick!"

Fuzz said.

"Just in case."

They found a big, long stick.

They ran back to Fuzz's yard.

"Where is it?" Cork asked.

"There," Fuzz whispered.

The pile of leaves wiggled.

Something under the leaves said,

"Chip-chip-chip!"

Fuzz lifted the stick over his head.

"Should I hit it?" he asked.

"No!" said Cork.

"First we need to see if it is

dangerous."

"Okay," said Fuzz.

"If it is not dangerous, I will keep it.
If it is dangerous, you can keep it."
Fuzz poked the end of the stick into
the pile of leaves.

"Chip-chip!"

Chomp!

"It chomped the end of the stick!"

Fuzz yelled.

"What do I do now?"

"Pull the stick out!" Cork said.

Fuzz pulled the stick out of the leaves.

A small, brown thing hung on the

end of the stick.

It hung on with its teeth.

Chapter 3

"It is a baby something!" Fuzz said.

"It is not a baby," Cork said.

"It is a chip-mouse."

Fuzz jiggled the stick.

The chipmunk bounced

on the end of it.

"He is cute and bouncy," Fuzz said.

"I think I will keep him!"

"You cannot keep a chip-mouse,"

Cork said.

"I found him," Fuzz said.

"I can keep him for a pet.

Finders keepers!"

"Oh, brother!" Cork said.

The chipmunk dropped to the ground.

"Chip-chip-chip!" he said.

He picked up a nut.

He stuck it in his cheek.

He picked up a berry.

He stuck it in his cheek.

He picked up a seed pod.

He stuck it in his cheek.

"Chip-chip-chip!"

"I wonder how much he can stuff in his cheeks," Cork said.

"We can find out," Fuzz said.

"We will help him."

Fuzz handed two nuts to the chipmunk.

23

The chipmunk stuffed them
into his cheeks.

Cork handed three berries
to the chipmunk.

The chipmunk stuffed them
into his cheeks.

The chipmunk's cheeks grew
fatter and fatter.

Fuzz opened his paw to pick up
another nut.

The shiny green stone fell
to the ground.

The chipmunk scooped it up and
stuffed it into his cheek.

"That is my stone!" Fuzz yelled.

"That is *my* stone!" Cork said.

"Chip-chip-chip!" said the chipmunk.

"I think he is saying 'finders
keepers,'" Cork said.

The chipmunk disappeared under
his lump of leaves with his cheeks
full of nuts and berries and the shiny
green stone.

Chapter 4

The chipmunk popped out of the
leaves with empty cheeks.

He ran back to the nut tree.

"Now my stone has chip-mouse spit on it," Cork said.

"I want it back anyway," Fuzz said.

Cork and Fuzz dug into the lump of leaves.

They found nuts and berries and seeds.

And they found the shiny green stone.

Fuzz grabbed it.

"Finders keepers," he said.

"CHIP-CHIP-CHIP-CHIP-CHIP!" the chipmunk yelled at them.

He jumped up and down.

He ran in circles, flicking his tail.

"I think he is mad at us," Fuzz said.

"I think we should go home now,"
Cork said.

Fuzz looked back at the chattering
chipmunk.

He sniffled.

"I wanted to keep that chip-mouse
for a pet," Fuzz said.

"Now I feel sad."

Cork put his arm around
his friend's shoulders.

"Sometimes we cannot keep
the things we find," Cork said.

"Sometimes they belong to someone
else."

"Who does the chip-mouse belong
to?" Fuzz asked.

"Well," said Cork, "I guess he just belongs to himself."

Fuzz looked at the green stone in his paw.

He gave it to Cork.

"You are right," Fuzz said.

"I cannot keep your green stone. Now I feel sadder."

"You can borrow my stone sometime," Cork said.

"And if it will make you feel better, we can see how many nuts we can stuff into our own cheeks."

And so they did.

Two best friends, arm in arm,

heading for home with fat, fat

cheeks.